THE FLOWER FAMILY

by Yutaka Sugita

McGraw-Hill Book Company

New York   St. Louis   San Francisco

Cataloging in Publication Data appears on last page.

100318

Two flowers grew side by side across the path from a pool in a tiny garden. One flower had pink petals with red tips. The other one had petals that were striped in violet and blue. The two flowers spent each day sunning cozily and gossiping together.

One afternoon while a breeze was gently ruffling their petals, the pink and red flower said to her neighbor:

"Do you suppose there are other flowers blooming beautifully like us?"

Her friend thought about it. Before she had a chance to say anything, she was surprised to feel the breeze suddenly grow stronger. Then the wind whispered:

"You two flowers are very beautiful indeed, but flowers grow everywhere – in the country and in cities, on deserts, on mountains and in fields – flowers grow wherever the earth is warmed by the sun and there is water. Why, I myself have carried their seeds to the North and the South, to the East and the West."

"Would you think a flower could grow on a railroad track? That's where I saw a bright red blossom one day."

"Oh..." said the violet and blue flower. But the wind went on: "In Southern lands and islands – wherever the sun is hot many months of the year – some flowers grow very big, almost as big as the flamingos who live there."

"If only you could come with me – I would show you pretty flowers poking out between sidewalk pavements – between rocks and bricks on walls – and on rooftops."

"Even in the far North where there are heavy snowfalls, the sun warms the earth long enough for boys and girls to find flowers to pick."

"Some flowers are planted carefully, as you were, in this nice garden."

"Oh..." the blue and violet flower tried once again to say something, but the wind didn't give her a chance to be heard.

"The seeds of other flowers are carried by the waters of rivers and lakes and ponds and by the sea," said the wind.

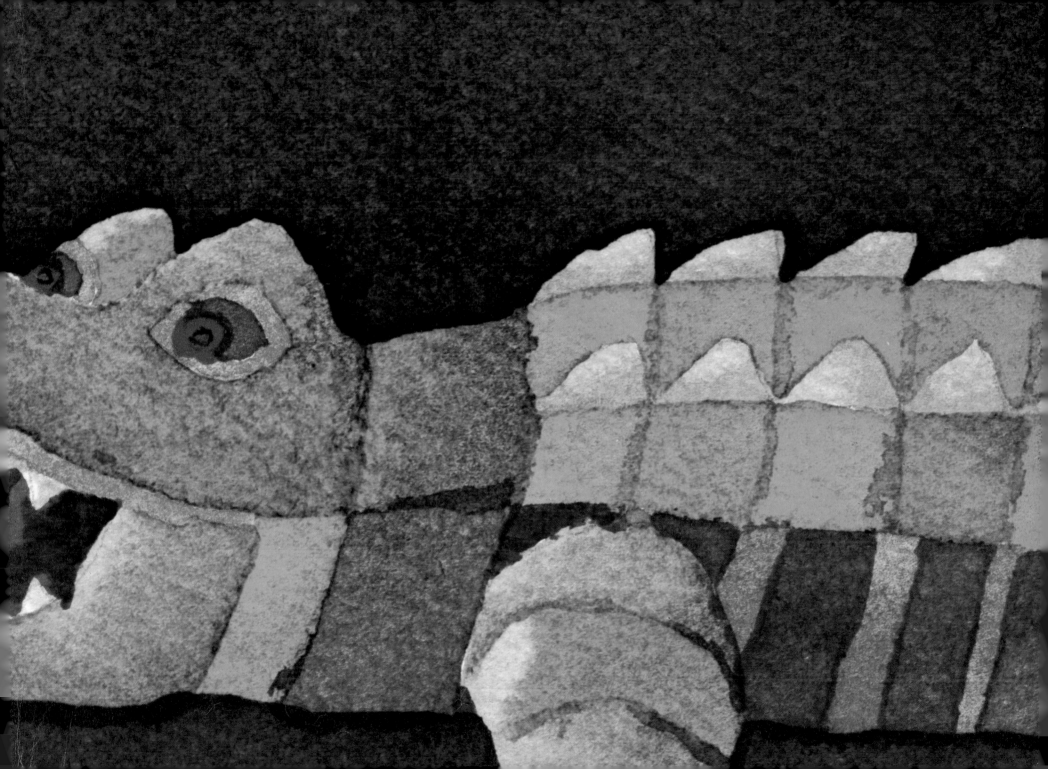

"Some flower seeds cling to the feathers of birds who drop them in flight. Other flower seeds are caught up on the shoes of boys and girls or on the paws of cats or dogs – or even the hoofs of camels! The seeds might take root wherever they fall."

"Wherever even one flower blooms, its soft perfume and lovely color brings happiness:

"To lonely island outposts –

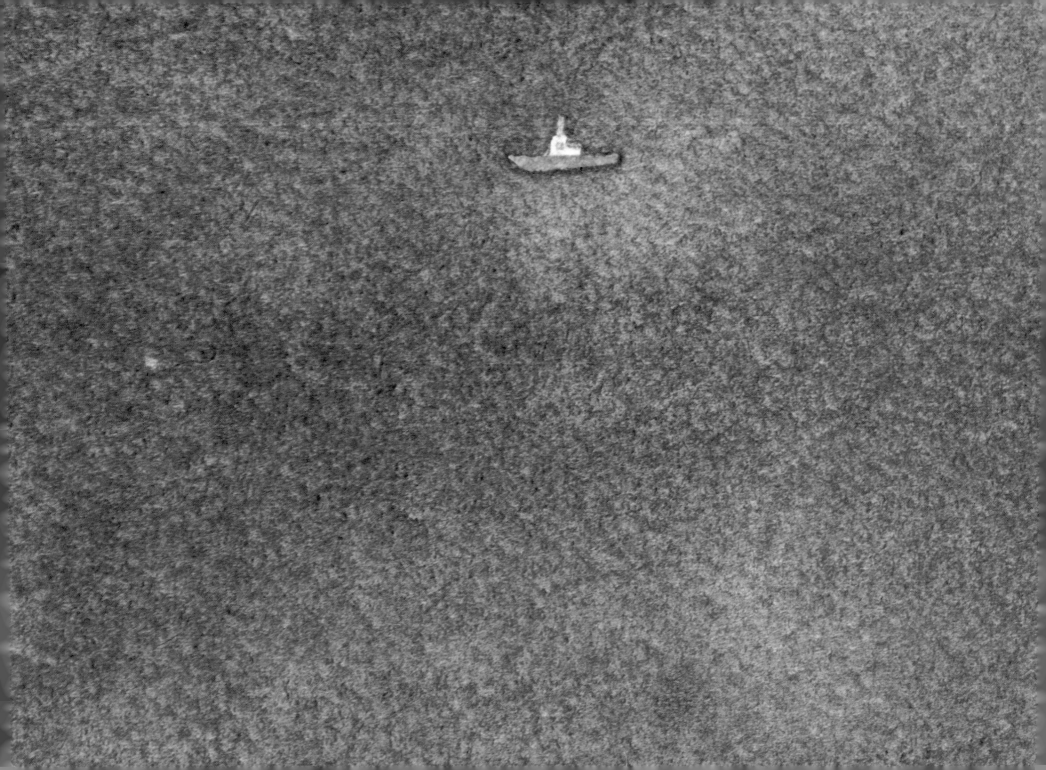

``To a small girl who is sick in bed —

"To nuns in a quiet convent –

All the members of the wonderful flower family, dressed in all colors of the rainbow, ring the world with beauty."

"Oh! What a lovely story," the blue and violet flower cried. "I couldn't tell it better myself. Thank you!"

And her neighbor nodded her pink and red petals happily in agreement.

Library of Congress Cataloging in Publication Data
Sugita, Yutaka,
   The flower family.
   SUMMARY: Flowers bloom all around the world
bringing cheer, beauty, and happiness wherever they
are found.
   [1. Flowers—Fiction] I. Title.
PZ7.S944Fl [E]   75-20082
ISBN 0-07-061768-6
ISBN 0-07-061769-4 lib. bdg.